Milly and Molly

For my grandchildren
Thomas, Harry, Ella and Madeleine

Milly, Molly and Alf

Copyright © Milly Molly Books, 2002

Gill Pittar and Cris Morrell assert the moral right to
be recognized as the author and illustrator of this
work.

Published by
Milly Molly Books
P O Box 539
Gisborne, New Zealand
email: books@millymolly.com

Printed by Rhythm Consolidated Berhad, Malaysia

ISBN: 1-86972-018-0

10   9   8   7   6   5   4   3 — 2   1

Milly, Molly
and
Alf

"We may look different
but we feel the same."

On an ordinary, hot summer day, the door to
Milly and Molly's classroom burst open and
in stepped the new boy.

Miss Blythe introduced Alf to the class.
"Alf is making a new start, in a new country,"
Miss Blythe explained. "Alf is a refugee.
His own country is not a safe place to live."

Milly and Molly offered to show Alf where
to put his things.

But Alf was different.

He didn't own a school bag or a bathing suit.

Alf kept an apple in his pocket and a pencil behind his ear.

And he wore his black pair of shorts
for everything.

Milly and Molly took an immediate liking
to Alf.

It didn't seem to matter that he never combed his hair and had no shoes.

He smelt deliciously soapy and was
never lost for words.

Alf lived in the caravan park with Nan.
She wasn't his mother and he didn't
have a father.

But Nan made the rules and Alf followed
them.

Milly and Molly were excited when Alf chose
them to be in his team on sports day.
He knew when to be quiet...

...and when to be noisy.

He didn't get cross and he didn't get flustered.
Before every race, Alf would say, "you can do it."
And they did. Milly, Molly and Alf won all
their races.

But Alf was different.
He didn't talk about his home and family
or Christmas and birthdays.
He didn't have a pet or a particular hobby.
He didn't share his thoughts or all his feelings.
Alf didn't cry and he didn't smile either.

When Miss Blythe asked hard questions
like, "who is the President of America"
or "what is the capital of South Africa?"
Alf always knew the answers.

"How do you know all that stuff?" Milly
and Molly asked.
"Nan reads me the newspaper," said Alf.

Alf always scored on top in spelling.
"How do you do it?" Milly and Molly asked.

"Sometimes, I help Nan with the crossword," said Alf.

$25 + 25 = 50$
$11 \times 10 = 110$
$10 - 5 = 5$
$20 \div 2 = 10$

$25 + 25 = 5$
$11 \times 10 = 1$
$10 - 5 =$

Alf always scored highest in math.
"Who taught you?" Milly and Molly asked.

"The butcher," said Alf. "I help him after
school for pocket money. If I'm quick with
my jobs he lets me help balance the drawer."

Prizegiving day

On the last day of school, Miss Blythe asked
Alf to stand up.

"Alf," she said, "you've been a pleasure to teach. But you've taught us lots more." Miss Blythe gave Alf the prize for 'Best All-Rounder'.

Suddenly ... Alf smiled.

What's more, he was lost for words.

Milly, Molly and Alf

The value implicitly expressed in this story is 'celebration of difference' - understanding, respecting and enjoying the difference of others.

Alf was different from everyone else in his class. Alf's difference and contribution was celebrated on Prizegiving day.

"We may look different but we feel the same."

BOOKS

Other picture books in the Milly, Molly series include:

- Milly, Molly and Jimmy's Seeds   ISBN 1-86972-000-8

- Milly, Molly and Beefy   ISBN 1-86972-006-7

- Milly, Molly and Pet Day   ISBN 1-86972-004-0

- Milly, Molly and Oink   ISBN 1-86972-002-4

- Milly and Molly Go Camping   ISBN 1-86972-003-2

- Milly, Molly and Betelgeuse   ISBN 1-86972-005-9

- Milly, Molly and Taffy Bogle   ISBN 1-86972-001-6

- Milly, Molly and Aunt Maude   ISBN 1-86972-014-8

- Milly, Molly and Sock Heaven   ISBN 1-86972-015-6

- Milly, Molly and the Sunhat   ISBN 1-86972-016-4

- Milly, Molly and Special Friends   ISBN 1-86972-017-2

- Milly, Molly and Different Dads   ISBN 1-86972-019-9